To Sophia- love from
Nora & Gordon
2015

Scary Fairy Tales

The Wicked Witch of the West

and other stories

Compiled by Vic Parker

Miles Kelly

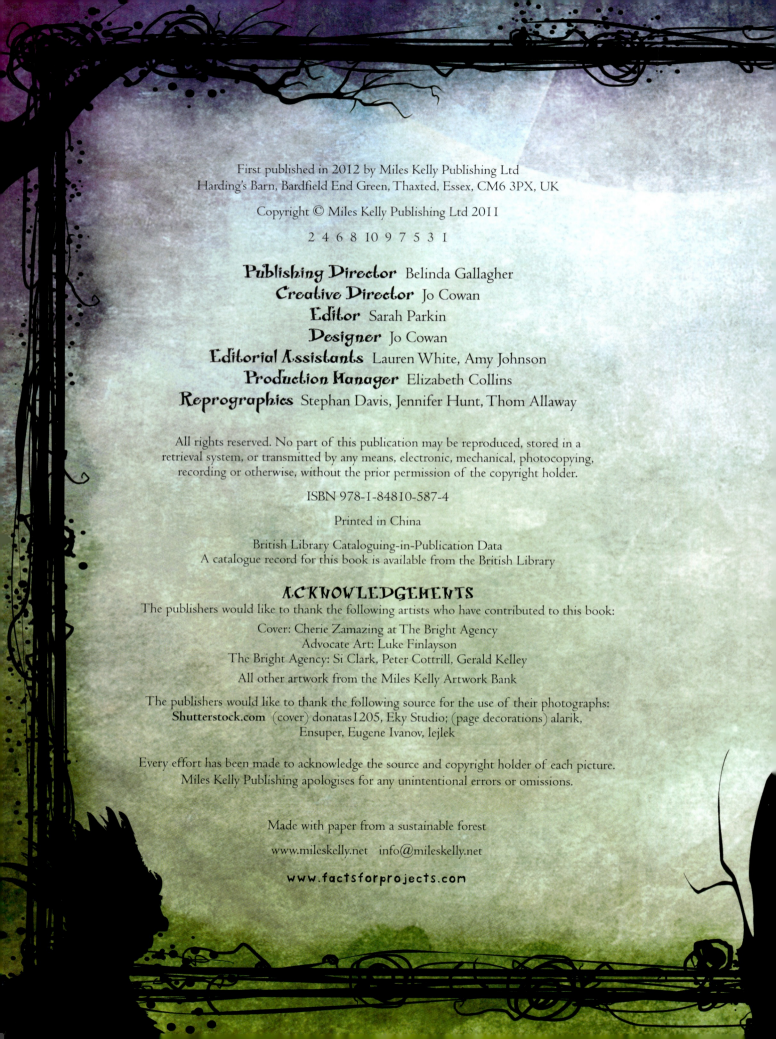

First published in 2012 by Miles Kelly Publishing Ltd
Harding's Barn, Bardfield End Green, Thaxted, Essex, CM6 3PX, UK

2 4 6 8 10 9 7 5 3 1

Publishing Director Belinda Gallagher
Creative Director Jo Cowan
Editor Sarah Parkin
Designer Jo Cowan
Editorial Assistants Lauren White, Amy Johnson
Production Manager Elizabeth Collins
Reprographics Stephan Davis, Jennifer Hunt, Thom Allaway

ISBN 978-1-84810-587-4

Printed in China

British Library Cataloguing-in-Publication Data
A catalogue record for this book is available from the British Library

ACKNOWLEDGEMENTS
The publishers would like to thank the following artists who have contributed to this book:

Cover: Cherie Zamazing at The Bright Agency
Advocate Art: Luke Finlayson
The Bright Agency: Si Clark, Peter Cottrill, Gerald Kelley

All other artwork from the Miles Kelly Artwork Bank

The publishers would like to thank the following source for the use of their photographs:
Shutterstock.com (cover) donatas1205, Eky Studio; (page decorations) alarik,
Ensuper, Eugene Ivanov, lejlek

Every effort has been made to acknowledge the source and copyright holder of each picture.
Miles Kelly Publishing apologises for any unintentional errors or omissions.

Made with paper from a sustainable forest

www.mileskelly.net   info@mileskelly.net

www.factsforprojects.com

Contents

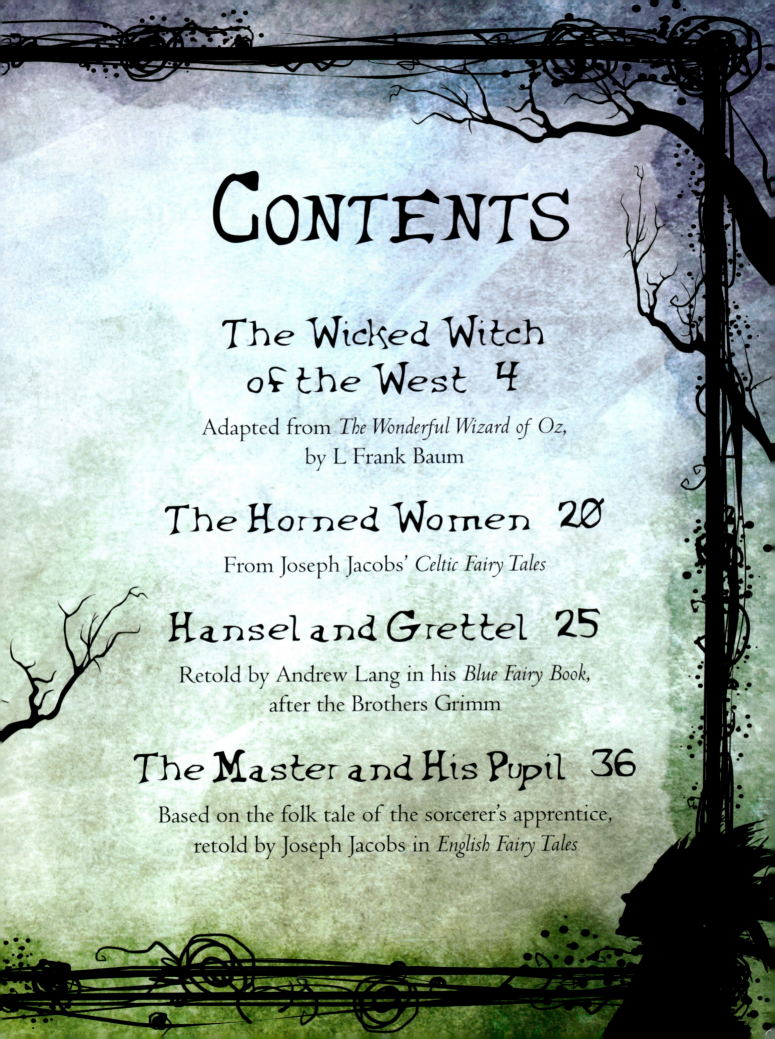

The Wicked Witch of the West

Adapted from *The Wonderful Wizard of Oz*,
by L Frank Baum

Dorothy lives in a farmhouse in Kansas, which is one day whisked into the air by a tornado — with her and her little dog Toto inside. It drops down into the Land of Oz, where Dorothy meets the Good Witch of the North, who gives her some silver shoes and tells her that to return home, she must go to the Emerald City and ask the Wizard of Oz for help. Dorothy travels down the Yellow Brick Road, befriending the Scarecrow, the Tin Woodman and the Cowardly Lion. They go with her, as the Scarecrow wants to ask the Wizard for a brain, the Tin Woodman for a heart, and the Cowardly Lion for some courage. When they finally reach the Wizard, he agrees to help them — but only if they can kill the Wicked Witch of the West, who rules over the Winkie Country…

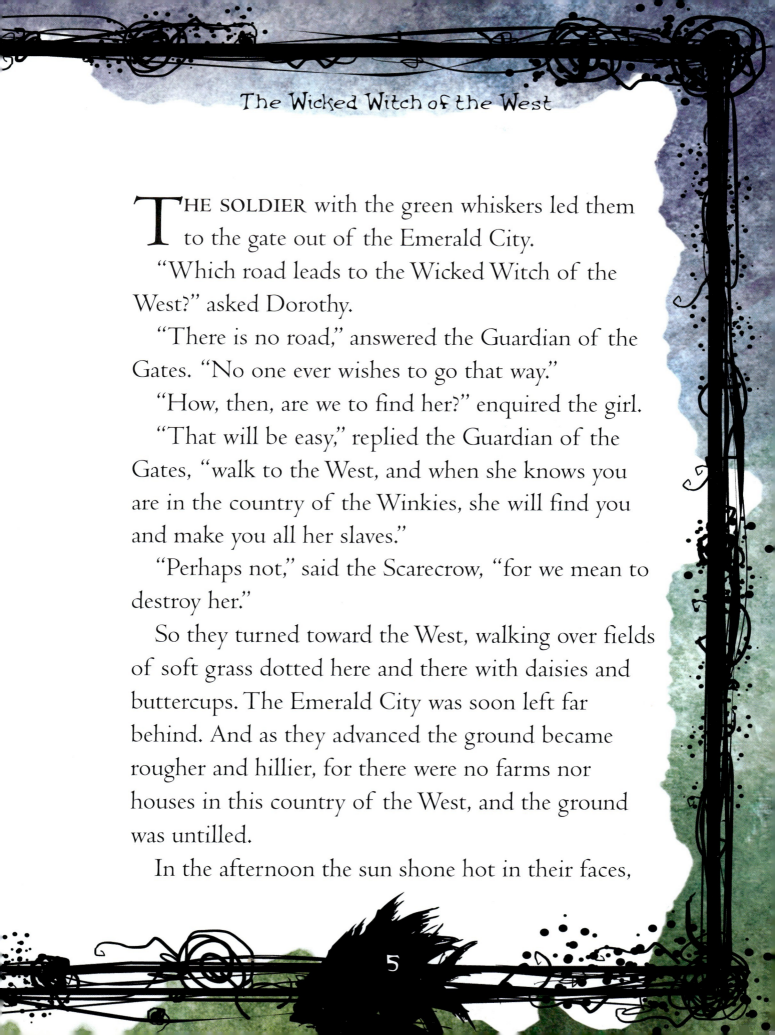

THE SOLDIER with the green whiskers led them to the gate out of the Emerald City.

"Which road leads to the Wicked Witch of the West?" asked Dorothy.

"There is no road," answered the Guardian of the Gates. "No one ever wishes to go that way."

"How, then, are we to find her?" enquired the girl.

"That will be easy," replied the Guardian of the Gates, "walk to the West, and when she knows you are in the country of the Winkies, she will find you and make you all her slaves."

"Perhaps not," said the Scarecrow, "for we mean to destroy her."

So they turned toward the West, walking over fields of soft grass dotted here and there with daisies and buttercups. The Emerald City was soon left far behind. And as they advanced the ground became rougher and hillier, for there were no farms nor houses in this country of the West, and the ground was untilled.

In the afternoon the sun shone hot in their faces,

for there were no trees to offer them shade; so that before night Dorothy and Toto and the Lion were tired, and lay down upon the grass and fell asleep, with the Woodman and the Scarecrow keeping watch.

Now the Wicked Witch of the West had but one eye, yet that was as powerful as a telescope, and could see everywhere. So, as she sat in the door of her castle, she happened to look around and saw Dorothy lying asleep, with her friends all about her. They were a long distance off, but the Wicked Witch was angry to find them in her country; so she blew upon a silver whistle that hung around her neck.

At once there came running to her from all directions a pack of great wolves. They had long legs and fierce eyes and sharp teeth.

"Go to those people," said the Witch, "and tear them to pieces."

"Are you not going to make them your slaves?" asked the leader of the wolves.

"No," the Witch answered, "one is of tin, and one of straw; one is a girl and another a lion. None of them is fit to work, so you may tear them all into small pieces."

"Very well," said the wolf, and he dashed away at full speed, followed by the others.

It was lucky the Scarecrow and the Woodman were wide awake and heard the wolves coming.

"This is my fight," said the Woodman, "so get behind me and I will meet them as they come."

He seized his axe, which he had made very sharp, and as the leader of the wolves came on the Tin Woodman swung his arm and chopped the wolf's

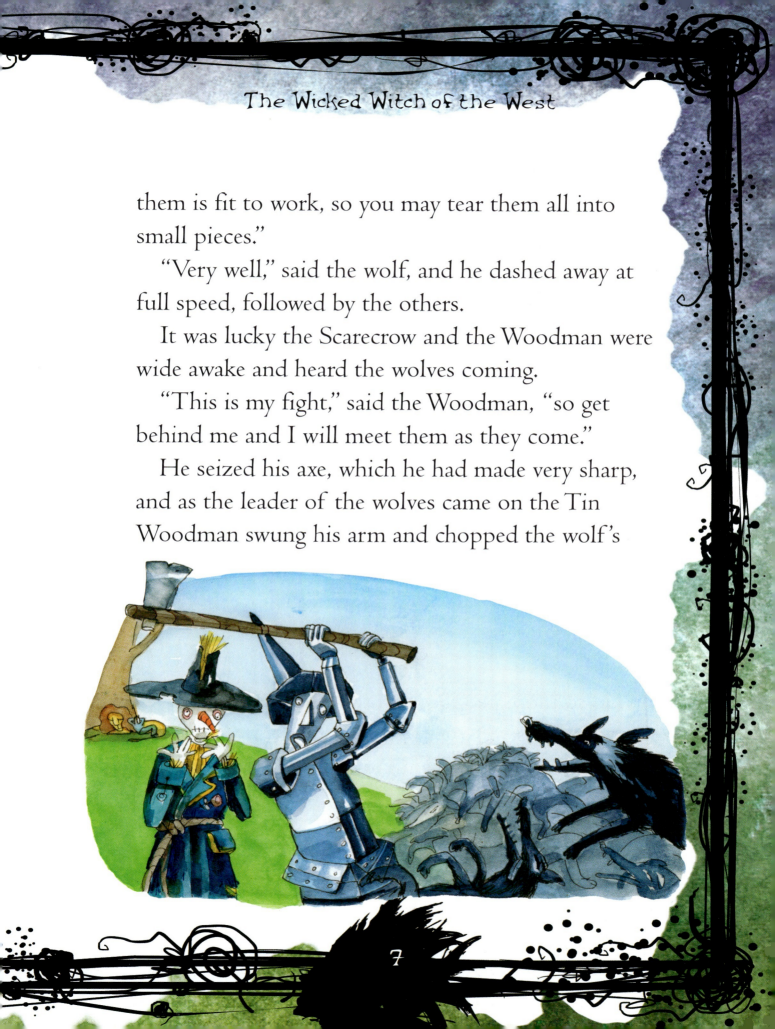

head from its body, so that it immediately died. As soon as he could raise his axe another wolf came up, and he also fell under the sharp edge of the Tin Woodman's weapon. There were forty wolves, and forty times a wolf was killed, so that at last they all lay dead in a heap before the Woodman.

Then he put down his axe and sat beside the Scarecrow, who said, "It was a good fight, friend."

They waited until Dorothy awoke the next morning. The little girl was quite frightened when she saw the great pile of shaggy wolves, but the Tin Woodman told her all. She thanked him for saving them and sat down to breakfast, after which they started again upon their journey.

Now this same morning the Wicked Witch came to the door of her castle and looked out with her one eye that could see far off. She saw all her wolves lying dead, and the strangers still travelling through her country. This made her angrier than before, and she blew her silver whistle twice.

A great flock of wild crows came flying toward her,

enough to darken the sky.

And the Wicked Witch said to the King Crow, "Fly to the strangers; peck out their eyes and tear them to pieces."

The wild crows flew in one great flock toward Dorothy and her companions. When the little girl saw them coming she was afraid.

But the Scarecrow said, "This is my battle, so lie down beside me all of you and you will not be harmed."

So they all lay upon the ground

except the Scarecrow, and he stood up and stretched out his arms. And when the crows saw him they were frightened, as these birds always are by scarecrows, and did not dare to come any nearer. But the King Crow said: "It is only a stuffed man. I will peck his eyes out."

The King Crow flew at the Scarecrow, who caught it by the head and twisted its neck until it died. And then another crow flew at him, and the Scarecrow twisted its neck also. Soon there were forty crows, and forty times the Scarecrow twisted a neck, until at last all were lying dead beside him. Then he called to his companions to rise, and again they started upon their journey.

When the Wicked Witch looked out again and saw all her crows lying in a heap, she got into a terrible rage, and blew three times upon her silver whistle.

Forthwith there was heard a great buzzing in the air, and a swarm of black bees came flying toward her.

"Go to the strangers and sting them to death!" commanded the Witch, and the bees turned and flew

rapidly until they came to where Dorothy and her friends were walking. But the Woodman had seen them coming, and the Scarecrow had decided what to do.

"Take out my straw and scatter it over the little girl and the dog and the Lion," he said to the Woodman, "then the bees will not be able to sting them." This the Woodman did, and as Dorothy lay close beside the Lion and held Toto in her arms, the straw covered them entirely.

The bees came and found no one but the Woodman to sting, so they flew at him and broke off all their stings against the tin, without hurting the Woodman at all. And as bees cannot live when their stings are broken, that was the end of the black bees, and they lay scattered thick about the Woodman, like little heaps of fine coal.

Then Dorothy and the Lion got up, and the girl helped the Tin Woodman put the straw back into the Scarecrow again, until he was as good as ever. So they started upon their journey once more.

The Wicked Witch was so angry when she saw her black bees in little heaps like fine coal that she stamped her foot and tore her hair and gnashed her teeth. And then she called a dozen of her slaves, who were the Winkies, and gave them sharp spears, telling them to go to the strangers and destroy them.

The Winkies were not a brave people, but they had to do as they were told. So they marched away until they came near to Dorothy. Then the Lion gave a great roar and sprang towards them, and the poor Winkies were so frightened that they ran back as fast as they could.

When they returned to the castle the Wicked Witch beat them well with a strap, and sent them back to their work, after which she sat down to think what she should do next. She could not understand how all her plans to destroy these strangers had failed; but she was a powerful witch, as well as a wicked one, and she soon made up her mind how to act.

There was, in her cupboard, a Golden Cap, with a circle of diamonds and rubies running round it. This Golden Cap had a charm. Whoever owned it could call three times upon the Winged Monkeys, who would obey any order they were given. But no person could command these strange creatures more than three times. Twice already the Wicked Witch had used the charm of the Cap. Once was when she had made the Winkies her slaves, and set herself to rule over their country. The Winged Monkeys had helped her do this. The second time was when she had fought against the Great Oz himself, and driven him out of the land of the West. The Winged Monkeys had also helped her in doing this. Only once more could she use this Golden Cap, for which reason she did not like to do so until all her other powers were exhausted. But now that her wolves and her crows and her bees were gone, and her slaves had been scared away by the Cowardly Lion, she saw there was only one way left to destroy Dorothy and her friends.

So the Wicked Witch took the Golden Cap and placed it on her head. Then she stood upon her left foot and said slowly: "Ep-pe, pep-pe, kak-ke!"

Next she stood upon her right foot and said: "Hil-lo, hol-lo, hel-lo!"

After this she stood upon both feet and cried in a loud voice: "Ziz-zy, zuz-zy, zik!"

The charm began to work. The sky darkened and a rumbling sound was heard. There was a rushing of wings, a chattering and laughing, and the sun came out to show the Wicked Witch surrounded by monkeys, each with a pair of wings on his shoulders.

One, the leader, and bigger than the others, flew down to the Witch and said, "You have called us for the third and last time. What do you command?"

"Go to the strangers who are within my land and destroy them all except the Lion," said the Wicked Witch. "Bring that beast to me, for I have a mind to harness him like a horse, and make him work."

"Your commands shall be obeyed," said the big monkey. Then, with a great deal of chattering and noise, the huge crowd of Winged Monkeys flew away to find the place where Dorothy and her three friends were walking.

Some of the monkeys seized the Tin Woodman and carried him through the air until they were over a country that was thickly covered with sharp rocks. Here they dropped the poor Woodman, who fell a great distance to the rocks, where he lay so battered and dented that he could neither move nor groan.

Some other monkeys caught the Scarecrow, and with their long fingers pulled all of the straw out of his clothes and head. They made his hat and boots and clothes into a small bundle and threw it into the top branches of a tall tree.

The remaining monkeys threw pieces of stout rope

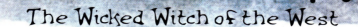

around the Lion and wound many coils about his body and head and legs, until he was unable to bite or scratch or struggle in any way. Then they lifted him up and flew away with him to the Witch's castle, where he was placed in a small yard with a high iron fence around it, so that he could not escape.

But Dorothy they did not harm at all. She stood, with Toto in her arms, watching the awful fate of all her comrades and thinking it would soon be her turn. The leader of the Winged Monkeys flew up to her, his long, hairy arms stretched out and his ugly, cruel face grinning terribly; but then he saw the mark of the Good Witch's kiss upon Dorothy's forehead and stopped at once, motioning the other monkeys not to touch her.

"We cannot harm this little girl," he ordered them, "for look, she has the protection of the Power of Good, and that is far, far greater than the Power of Evil. The very most we can do is to transport her with care to the castle of the Wicked Witch and leave her there."

So, carefully and gently, they lifted Dorothy in their arms and carried her swiftly through the air until they came to the castle, where they set her down upon the front doorstep. Then the leader said to the Witch: "We have obeyed you as far as we were able. Your power over our band is now ended, and you will never see us again." Then all the Winged Monkeys, with much laughing and chattering and noise, flew into the air and were soon out of sight.

The Wicked Witch looked down at Dorothy's feet, and seeing the Silver Shoes, began to tremble with fear, for she knew what a powerful charm belonged to them. But then she looked into the child's eyes and saw that the little girl did not know of the wonderful power the Silver Shoes gave her. So the Wicked Witch laughed to herself, and said to Dorothy, very harshly and severely: "Come with me little girl; and see that you listen carefully to everything I tell you, for if you do not I will surely make an end of you, as I did of the Tin Woodman and the Scarecrow."

So Dorothy became a slave for the Wicked Witch, and realised that it would be harder than ever to get back to Kansas again.

The Horned Women

From Joseph Jacobs' *Celtic Fairy Tales*

A RICH WOMAN sat up late one night carding wool, while all the family and servants were asleep. Suddenly there came a knock at the door and a voice outside called, "Open! Open!"

"Who is there?" said the woman of the house.

"I am the Witch of one Horn," came the answer.

The mistress opened the door and a woman with a horn growing on her forehead entered, holding a pair of wool-carders. She sat down by the fire in silence, and began to card the wool with violent haste. Suddenly she paused, and said aloud: "Where are the women? They delay too long."

Then a second knock came to the door, and a voice called, "Open! Open!"

The mistress felt herself obliged to rise and open the door, and immediately a second witch entered, having two horns on her forehead, and in her hand a wheel for spinning wool.

"Give me place," she said; "I am the Witch of two Horns," and she began to spin as quick as lightning. And so the knocks went on, and the call was heard, and the witches entered, until at last twelve women sat round the fire — the first with one horn, the last with twelve horns. And they carded the thread, and turned their spinning-wheels, and wound and wove,

all singing together an ancient rhyme, but they didn't speak a word to the mistress of the house. Strange to hear and frightful to look upon were these twelve women, with their horns and their wheels. The mistress was frightened to death and tried to get up to call for help, but she could not move, nor could she utter a word or a cry, for the spell of the witches was upon her.

Then one of them called to her, "Rise and make us a cake."

Then the mistress searched for a jug to bring water from the well that she might make the cake mix, but she couldn't find one.

And the witches said to her, "Take a sieve and bring water in it."

So she took the sieve and went to the well; but the water poured through the holes, and she sat down by the well and wept.

Then a voice from the well said, "Take yellow clay and moss, and bind them together, and plaster the sieve so that it will hold."

This she did, and the sieve held the water.

Then the voice said again: "Go back to the house, and just before you enter, cry aloud three times, 'The mountain and the sky over it is all on fire'."

And she did so.

When the witches inside heard the call, a great and terrible cry broke from their lips, and they rushed forth with wild shrieks, and fled away back home.

Then the Spirit of the Well told the mistress of the house to enter and prepare her home against the enchantments of the witches if they returned again.

First, to break their spells, she sprinkled the water in which she had washed her child's feet, outside the door. Secondly, she took the cake which in her absence the witches had made of meal mixed with blood drawn from her sleeping family, and she broke the cake in bits, and placed a bit in the mouth of each sleeper, and they woke up, free from the witches' power. Lastly, she secured the door with a great crossbeam barred against it, so that the witches could not enter. Having done these things she waited.

The witches weren't long in coming back, and they raged and called for vengeance.

"Open! Open!" they screamed. "Open, feet-water!"

"I cannot," said the feet-water; "I am scattered on the ground, trickling away to the lake."

"Open, open, wood and trees and beam!" they cried to the door.

"I cannot," said the door, "for I am fixed and have no power to move."

"Open, open, cake that we have made and mingled with blood!" they cried again.

"I cannot," said the cake, "for I am completely broken and bruised."

Then the witches rushed through the air with great cries, and fled back home, uttering strange curses on the Spirit of the Well, who had wished their ruin. And the mistress and the house were left in peace.

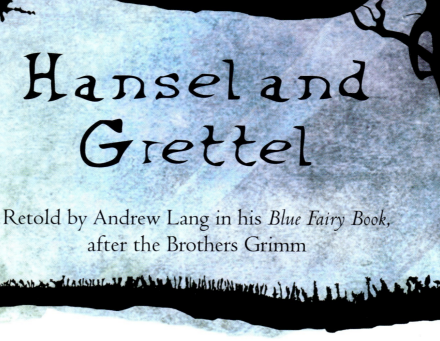

Hansel and Grettel

Retold by Andrew Lang in his *Blue Fairy Book*,
after the Brothers Grimm

ONCE UPON A TIME there dwelt on the outskirts of a large forest a poor woodcutter with his wife and two children; the boy was called Hansel and the girl, Grettel. He had always little to live on, and a time came when he couldn't even provide them with daily bread. One night, unable to sleep with worry, he sighed and said to the children's stepmother: "What's to become of us? How are we to live?"

"I'll tell you what, husband," answered the woman, "early tomorrow morning we'll take the children out into the thickest part of the wood and leave them."

"No, wife," said her husband, "how could I!"

"Then we must all four die of hunger," said she, and she nagged and moaned till he agreed.

The children had been awake with hunger and had heard everything. Grettel wept bitterly, but Hansel got up, slipped on his coat, opened the back door and stole out. The moon was shining and the white pebbles which lay in front of the house glittered like silver. Hansel filled his pocket with as many of them as he could. Then he went back and said to Grettel: "Be comforted, my dear little sister, and go to sleep: I have a way to escape."

At daybreak, the woman came and woke the children. "Get up, we're all going to fetch wood," she commanded. She gave them each a bit of bread and said: "There's something for your lunch — it's all you're getting." Then they all set out together.

After they had walked for a little, Hansel stood and looked back at the house, and this he repeated again and again. His father observed him, and said: "Hansel, what are you gazing at?"

"Oh Father," said Hansel, "I am looking back at

my white kitten, which is sitting on the roof, waving me farewell." However Hansel had not looked back at his kitten, but each time had dropped one of the white pebbles out of his pocket on to the path.

When they had reached the middle of the forest and collected brushwood for a fire the woman said: "Now sit down, children, and rest: we are going to cut wood, but when we've finished we'll come back and fetch you."

Hansel and Grettel sat down beside the fire, and at midday ate their little bits of bread. When they had waited for a long time their eyes closed and they fell fast asleep.

It was pitch dark when they awoke. Grettel began to cry, and said: "How are we ever going to get out of the wood?"

But Hansel comforted her, saying, "Only wait, Grettel, till the full moon is up."

Then, he took his sister by the hand and followed the pebbles, which shone like bright coins in the moonlight and showed them the path. They walked

on through the night, and at daybreak reached their home again — to the stepmother's great annoyance and the father's huge relief.

Not long afterwards, one night the children again overheard their stepmother force their father to agree to abandon them in the forest. Hansel got up and wanted to go out and pick up pebbles again, as he had done the first time; but the woman had barred the door, and he couldn't get out.

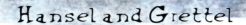

At early dawn the woman came and made the children get up. They received their bit of bread, but it was even smaller than before. On the way into the wood Hansel crumbled it in his pocket, and every few minutes he stood still and dropped a crumb on the ground. "Hansel, what are you stopping and looking about for?" said the father.

"I'm looking back at my little pigeon, which is sitting on the roof waving me farewell," answered Hansel. But Hansel was gradually throwing all his crumbs on the path.

The woman led the children still deeper into the forest. Then a big fire was lit again, and she said: "Just sit down there, children; we're going into the forest to cut down wood, and in the evening when we're finished we'll come back to fetch you."

At midday Grettel divided her bread with Hansel, for he had strewn his all along their path. Then they fell asleep and didn't awake till it was pitch dark and they were still all alone. Hansel comforted his sister, saying: "Only wait, Grettel, till the moon rises, then we shall see the breadcrumbs I scattered along the path; they will show us the way back to the house." When the moon appeared they got up, but they found no crumbs, for the birds had picked them all up. "Never mind," said Hansel to Grettel, "you'll see we'll find a way out;" but all the same they did not. They wandered about the whole night, and the next day, but they could not find a path out of the wood. They were very hungry, too, for they had nothing to eat but a few berries they found.

On the third morning they got deeper and deeper into the wood, and now they felt that if help did not come to them soon they must perish. At midday they stumbled across a little house, and when they came quite near they saw that it was made of bread and roofed with cakes, while the windows were made of transparent sugar. Hansel stretched up his hand and broke off a little bit of the roof to see what it was like, and Grettel went to the window and began to nibble at it.

Suddenly the door opened, and an ancient dame

leaning on a staff hobbled out. Hansel and Grettel were terrified, but the old woman said: "Oh, ho! You dear children, come in and stay with me, no ill shall befall you." She took them both by the hand and let them into the house, and laid a most sumptuous dinner before them – milk and sugared pancakes, with apples and nuts. After they had finished, two beautiful little white beds were prepared for them, and when Hansel and Grettel lay down in them they felt as if they had got into heaven.

The old woman had appeared to be most friendly, but she was really an old witch who had only built the little bread house in order to lure the children in. For when anyone came into her power she killed, cooked, and ate him!

Early in the morning, before the children were awake, she rose up, and seized Hansel with her bony hand and carried him into a stable, and barred the door on him; he might scream as much as he liked, it did him no good. Then she went to Grettel, shook her awake and cried: "Get up, you lazy-bones, fetch

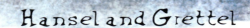

water and cook something for your brother. When he's fat I'll eat him up." Grettel began to cry bitterly, but it was no use; she had to do what the wicked witch bade her.

So the best food was cooked for poor Hansel, but Grettel got nothing but crab-shells. Every morning the old woman hobbled out to the stable and cried: "Hansel, put out your finger, that I may feel if you are getting fat." But Hansel always stretched out a bone, and the old dame, whose eyes were dim, couldn't see it. The witch always thought it was Hansel's finger and wondered why he fattened so slowly. When four weeks had passed and Hansel still remained thin, she lost patience and decided to wait no longer.

"Grettel," she called, "be quick and get some water. Hansel may be fat or thin, I'm going to kill him tomorrow and cook him."

Oh, how the poor little sister sobbed! Early in the morning she had to go out and hang up the kettle full of water and light the fire. "First we'll bake," said the old dame; "I've heated the oven already and kneaded the dough." She pushed Grettel out to the blazing oven. "Creep in," said the witch, "and see if it's hot enough, so that we can shove in the bread." For when she had got Grettel in she meant to close the oven and let the girl bake, that she might eat her up too.

But Grettel knew what she had in mind, and said: "I don't know how I'm to do it; how do I get in?"

"You silly goose!" said the hag. "The opening is big enough; see, I could get in myself," and she crawled toward it and poked her head into the oven. Then Grettel shoved her right in, shut the iron door, and drew the bolt. Gracious, how she yelled! It was quite horrible; but Grettel fled, and the wretched old woman was left to perish miserably.

Grettel flew straight to Hansel, opened the stable-door, and cried: "Hansel, we are free; the old witch is dead." Then Hansel sprang like a bird out of an opened cage. How they rejoiced, and jumped for joy, and kissed one another! They went back into the old hag's house, and here they found, in every corner of the room, boxes with pearls and precious stones, which they crammed into their clothes.

"Now," said Hansel, "let's get well away."

When they had wandered about for some hours, the wood became more and more familiar to them, and at length they saw their father's house in the distance. Then they set off to run and, bounding into the room, fell on their father with joy. He had been despairing since he left them in the wood, and the wicked stepmother had died. Grettel shook out her apron so that the pearls and precious stones rolled about the room, and Hansel threw down one handful after the other out of his pocket. Thus all their troubles were ended, and they lived happily ever after.

The Master and His Pupil

Based on the folk tale of the sorcerer's apprentice,
retold by Joseph Jacobs in *English Fairy Tales*

THERE WAS ONCE a very learned man in the
north-country who knew all the languages under
the sun, and who was acquainted with all the
mysteries of creation. He had one big book bound in
black leather and clasped with iron, and chained to a
table which was made fast to the floor. When he read
out of this book, he unlocked it with an iron key, and
none but he read from it, for it contained all the
secrets of the spirit world. It told how many angels
there were in heaven, and how they marched in their
ranks, and sang in their choirs, and what their names
and jobs were. And it told of the demons, how many

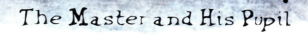

there were, and what their names and powers were, and how they might be summoned, and made to do people's bidding.

Now the master had a pupil who was but a foolish lad. He acted as a servant, and was never allowed to look into the black book, or hardly to enter the private room.

One day the master was out, and the lad, as curious as could be, hurried to the magical chamber. He gazed at his master's wondrous apparatus for changing copper into gold and lead into silver, and the mirror in which his master could see all that was passing in the world, and the shell which whispered to his master what people were saying at that very moment. However the lad realised he could do nothing with these things. "I don't know the right words to utter," he sighed. "They are locked up in the big black book."

He looked round and saw that the book was unfastened! The master had forgotten to lock it before he went out. The boy rushed to it and opened the volume. It was written with red-and-black ink, and much of it he could not understand; but he put his finger on a line and spelled it through.

At once the room was darkened, and the house trembled; a clap of thunder rolled through the passage and the old room, and there stood before him a horrible, horrible form, breathing fire, and with eyes like burning lamps. It was the demon Beelzebub, whom he had called up to serve him.

"Set me a task!" bellowed Beelzebub, with a voice like the roaring of an iron furnace.

The boy only trembled, and his hair stood up.

"Set me a task, or I shall strangle thee!"

But the lad could not speak.

Then the evil spirit stepped towards him, and putting forth his hands, touched his throat. The fingers burned his flesh. "Set me a task!"

"Water that flower over there," cried the boy in despair, pointing to a geranium which stood in a pot on the floor.

Instantly the spirit left the room, but in another instant he returned with a barrel on his back, and poured its contents over the flower; and again and again he went and came, and poured more and more water, till it was ankle-deep on the floor of the room.

"Enough, enough!" gasped the lad, but the demon heeded him not; the lad didn't know the words by which to send him away, and still he fetched water.

It rose to the boy's knees and still more water was poured. It mounted to his waist, and Beelzebub still kept on bringing barrels full. It rose to his armpits, and he scrambled to the table-top. And now the water in the room stood up to the window and washed against the glass, and swirled around his feet on the table. It still rose; it reached his breast. In vain he

cried; the evil spirit would not be dismissed, and to this day he would have been pouring water, and would have drowned all the world. But the master remembered on his journey that he had not locked his book, and therefore returned. At the moment when the water was bubbling about the pupil's chin, he rushed into the room and spoke the words which cast Beelzebub back into his fiery home.